This book belongs to

_____

Hair Like Mine

by
LaTashia M. Perry

Illustrator: Brittany J. Jackson

Publisher: G Publishing LLC

ISBN: 978-1-7340865-5-3

Library of Congress Control Number: 2015909238

Dedication

This book is dedicated to my beautiful curly haired babies, Cassidy Marie and Carrington Noel. To all the curly girls around the world, this book is for you also.

Hair Like Mine

Mama I've been searching
and I can't find anyone with Hair Like Mine.

Well honey,
that's because no two people are the same.
Everyone has different hair, nose, eyes, and toes.

I thought... what about
Gabby and Makenzie?
They look the same.

Well, except that Gabby's face is round
and hair is wavy and brown.

So I guess she's right about them.

But, what about Cameron and Aleah?
They look the same.

Well, except that they have a different frame.
Aleah is tall and Cameron is very small.

Okay she got me there.
I'm sure this can't be right.

No two people are exactly alike?

I searched all around

I was sure I could find someone
with Hair Like Mine.

I only found no two people
are the same.

Everyone has different hair,
nose, eyes, and toes.

Then I saw twins Adam and Aaron and they look exactly the same.

In fact it was hard to tell them apart.

But wait...
the closer I got
I could see that it's
true, even twins can be
different too?!?!

Aaron has hazel colored eyes and a few freckles
around his nose. Their hair was nothing alike,
they even have different toes!

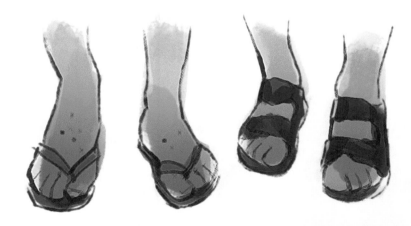

How could this be, even twins aren't the same.
This is all completely insane.

I felt defeated. I told mama she was right.
Not a single person was the same,
not one in sight.

I tried to find someone with Hair Like Mine,
I was sure that I could.
I don't like being different it doesn't feel good.
My hair is curly and really frizzy too;
It shrinks up way high,
this hair just won't do.

Honey I told you,
no two people are the same.

Everyone has different hair, nose,
eyes, and toes.

Even you and I are
different you see, my hair
is a lot more curly.

We are different shades of
brown and your eyes are a
bit more round;

you have a little button
nose

and look at your feet,
those are your father's
toes.

I know it's hard to understand now
but just wait you'll see,
how amazing being different can be.

There's no one in the world
quite like you. You're unique and beautiful.

As I laid in bed that night I thought,
maybe she's right.
It's kind of cool to know
there's only one me in sight.

I love my skin, my nose, eyes, and toes
And this Hair of Mine...
I like it just fine.

LaTashia M. Perry has a strong passion for encouraging and empowering young girls and women to love themselves just as they were created. She is very active in her community, starting the natural hair platform Secret Life of Curls. This was created to support and aid women and their children on their natural hair journey. LaTashia continues her work by hosting events, tackling topics such as self love, body image, and self esteem; never turning down an invite to speak at churches, women empowerment seminars, schools, and other community events.

In her spare time she enjoys spending time with her husband and their 5 children, traveling outside of their hometown located in Michigan.

To connect with the author visit:
www.4kidslikemine.com
Instagram: @4kidslikemine
Facebook: 4 Kids Like Mine
Email: 4kidslikemine@gmail

CPSIA information can be obtained
at www.ICGtesting.com
Printed in the USA
LVHW071540221020
669544LV00001B/7